Dad went to the building site.
He took Wilf and Wilma.

They looked at the crane.

Wilma spoke to the man in the cab.

A van came to the building site.

It had a weather vane on the back.

Wilf looked at the weather vane.

Dad had an idea.

Wilf jumped over the weather vane.

'Be careful,' said Dad.

'Take a photograph,' said Wilma.

She jumped over the weather vane.

The weather vane went on the roof.

Wilf took a photograph.

'See the weather vane,' said Wilf.
'We've jumped over it,' said Wilma.

'What a tall story!' said Biff.

But Wilf had a photograph.
'See,' he said.